Nita walked away from her family when she was seventeen years old, determined to never look back. But forty years later, when her mother died and her father descended into Alzheimer's, Nita returned to New Orleans to care for him in his final months.

Now her father has passed on, leaving to Nita her childhood home as an inheritance. But she soon finds she isn't the only resident. The house is occupied by ghosts of her past, playing out scenes of the life she fled.

What are they trying to tell her? Will they ever leave her in peace? And are they really spirits, or only visions, emerging from sealed-off depths of memory as from the shell of a chambered nautilus?

Novels by Anne L. Watson

Departure
A Chambered Nautilus
Flight
Joy
Pacific Avenue
Skeeter: A Cat Tale

THE ISLAND WOMEN TRILOGY
Cassie's Castaways
Willow's Crystal
Benecia's Mirror

ANNE L. WATSON

A Chambered Nautilus

Shepard & Piper
Bellingham, Washington

Library of Congress subject headings:
Family secrets—Fiction
Apparitions—Fiction
New Orleans (La.)—Fiction

Version 1.0

A Chambered Nautilus

1

The good part about inheriting my father's house in the suburbs of New Orleans, along with most of his money, was that I wouldn't have to rent anymore. Or go back to work. Being able to retire comfortably at the age of 58 was like winning the lottery.

The drawbacks were less obvious, but they showed up as time went by.

The first was predictable: Amanda and Louis, my older sister and younger brother, received only minor sums of money and a few keepsakes. They weren't silent about it, either.

Manda phoned shortly after she read her letter from Dad's lawyer. "Well, Nita, how'd you pull *that* off?" she asked. She didn't sound angry, more like she was asking for tips, in case she had a chance at a similar sly coup.

"I didn't pull anything off."

"He hadn't been competent for the last couple of years."

Oh? You knew?

I said, "You'll have to talk to a lawyer if you want to contest the will."

"Not me. I have better things to do."

"You do have two houses of your own, Manda. A summer one and a winter one, like dresses. Maybe he thought you didn't need a third."

"If you'd gone to college, maybe you wouldn't be so needy."

"There was that little matter of tuition."

"If you'd had the slightest idea what you wanted to do, maybe Dad would have paid for your college."

I drew a deep breath. Thought about trying to make her laugh. *If you hadn't hidden my Raggedy Ann in the garage when I was four, maybe I would have . . .*

No, it would probably misfire. "Manda, we can either quarrel over Dad's will or not. I'd rather not. The will was dated long before Alzheimer's took over his brain, and I don't think it was unfair, under the circumstances. I'd much, much rather be friends than enemies."

She was silent for a long few seconds. "Okay," she finally said. "Friends."

I hoped she meant it. We hadn't seen each other often, but she was the only one of the family who hadn't become a stranger. It's hard to lose the last one.

"Friends," I echoed.

When Lou called, he was even more direct. Right off, he asked, "Are you going to sell the house?"

"Hi, Lou," I said. "How are you? Haven't seen you in ages."

Like, haven't seen you helping with Dad's diapers for the past two years. Or even at the funeral. Possibly you were invisible, but I think you weren't here.

"Fine. I'm fine. Are you going to sell the house? Because if you do, you should split the money with Manda and me. Dad didn't know what he was doing at the end, as I'm sure you were well aware."

"I'm not selling it," I said. "I'm going to stay here. And before you say any more, check the date on your copy of the will. It was signed and witnessed at his lawyer's office long before his mind went. In fact, he did it while I was still in California."

He hung up on me.

Well, he'd get over it. Or, of course, maybe not.

The second drawback was that the house was haunted. Not by traditional misty, wailing ghosts. That might have been intriguing. No, it was haunted by the lives we'd lived there.

The first ghost—or whatever it was—appeared in the kitchen the morning after Dad's funeral.

A woman sprawls on the floor. Her hair hasn't been combed yet this morning, and her robe is hiked up around her thighs. Her head is turned so that her face isn't visible. A pan on the stove smokes dangerously.

I hadn't seen that when it happened. I'd imagined it when Dad called to tell me about Mom.

"Your mother died," he said.

My heart started pounding as if I'd run for a long time. "What happened?" I said.

"I don't know. She was making pancakes."

"And?" God, he was hard to talk to. At that point, I didn't know why.

"I smelled something burning."

Another full stop.

"And?"

"They said it was a heart attack."

"No."

That was all I could think to say. My mind went in a dozen directions. Images popped up in no particular order, some contradicting others. I imagined him frantically trying to revive her while the smoke alarm screamed. Or calmly leaning over her body to turn the burner off. Opening a window to let the smoke out. Calling 911. Pouring the pancake batter down the kitchen sink. Following the ambulance to the nearest hospital. Talking to paramedics, maybe police. I didn't ask for details. I didn't want to know.

"What can I do?" I asked.

"Nothing," he said.

"Do you need help?"

"No."

But he did. He had no idea how much help he needed. Mom had hidden his illness from us, maybe for years. It wouldn't have been hard to do. We weren't close, and he wasn't that bad yet. But when she was gone, there was no hiding anymore.

In the week after Dad's funeral, Mom's ghost was always there on the kitchen floor. After a while, she was still in the kitchen, but not dead anymore. Sometimes, she was happily making a birthday cake or a batch of her wonderful fudge. Washing fresh spinach at the sink. Making a pie from blackberries we'd picked. Singing, if you could call it that—she'd been tone-deaf. But her voice was music to her, and that's all that counted there in the kitchen.

Two little girls beg for tastes of frosting from the mixer beaters.

"Wait," their mother says. "You'll ruin your appetite for dinner. Wait and have the frosting on the cake."

"It's not as good on the cake," says Manda.

Their mother is surprised, even annoyed.

"It's the same frosting, and you'll have the cake, too. What do you mean, it's not as good?"

"Please, Mom? It's better when you just made it."

She gives them each a beater from the electric mixer. Not much frosting on either one, but exactly equal.

The girls are happy. It's only a little treat, a little indulgence, but it's enough.

Their mother frosts the cake quickly. As she turns to add the frosting bowl to the dishpan, she stumbles on a chair leg. The bowl slips out of her hand. Falling to the floor, it breaks.

"Oh!" she says furiously. "Why does everything always go wrong?"

2

It was my house now, and there was no lack of money. What would it take to banish the ghosts? Would new flooring do it? Would it take a whole kitchen remodel? What if I tore the house down—would that exact longitude and latitude ever be free?

Screwball idea.

There had to be a million other things to think about, and hundreds of things to do. Better to take care of the humdrum tasks and errands. Sitting around thinking about ghosts was a one-way ticket to the funny farm.

So I headed to the market. On foot, since I didn't drive. But I could learn now. I could call a driving school to give me lessons, and I had Dad's car. Most likely, it still ran. Or might. It had been years since anyone started it. I should get a mechanic to check it out.

Even in mid-morning, the sidewalk was beginning to shimmer with heat. Shade beckoned in the next block, where huge old oak trees on both sides made a dim vault over the street.

For some reason, this block always reminded me of the Miss America Pageant. Mom must have talked about it as we walked to school along that sidewalk. I'd never heard of the pageant before. I was outraged that she had not been declared the most beautiful woman in America. Someone had messed up, or someone had overlooked her, the way the prince had almost overlooked Cinderella when he came with the glass slipper. I fumed at the injustice of it.

Even after I was old enough to know that beauty pageants were corrupt and that my mother was a very ordinary woman, it was always the Miss America Block. And, long after I knew better, it reminded me that, at one time, I'd known my mother was the most wonderful woman in the world.

At least the interlaced trees made the walk cooler for one block. As I reemerged into the autumn inferno, I recalled the season in other places I'd lived. Cooler weather, blowing maple leaves. Not like the panting end of summer here in New Orleans, dreading the coming hurricane season.

Maybe I should carry an umbrella against the sun, the way Mom did. She popped them open at dogs, too, if they seemed threatening. Freaked them out completely. It was funny to think about, but loose dogs were a thing of the past. Even dogs had changed.

I passed my old school, which I would have avoided if I could. I hated that place. Even though it was a church school, it had been run by, and attended by, the most horrible people I'd known in my life.

I had no good memories of school. The first morning of kindergarten, Mom walked me to the schoolyard, put me through the gate, closed it, and walked away. I ran along my side of the chain link fence, trying to stay with her, until I reached the corner. As she crossed the street, merging into anonymous not-mothers, I clung to the fence and wailed. A year too young for kindergarten, I'd been admitted because I'd already taught myself to read. Regardless of that, I wasn't ready.

And the other children were not kind. Their contempt for the baby among them progressed from *nyaaah-nyaaah* teasing to snobbish shunning to sexual harassment as we reached our teens. But I had to go there because it was an all-white private school. Public schools were about to be integrated, and my parents refused to let us know black children. I often wondered how any child, of any race, could be worse than the bullies in that school.

So now I avoided that side of the street, looked away from the familiar brick building with its chain-link fence. I told myself that my tormentors had undoubtedly had their own tormentors, that no one escapes childhood unscathed. I focused on the houses across the street from the school, and walked on.

One more block, and then the market. During the years I'd been away, it had been remodeled and enlarged beyond recognition. Still, there was a neighborhood friendliness I wouldn't have found in a big-box store. Different owners now, the new ones Vietnamese. Now I was a regular, someone to be greeted by name, and perhaps given a small bonus, like a few herb sprigs to season the meat.

Today, Linh, the daughter of the family, gave me a sympathetic smile as I entered the store.

"I'm so sorry about your father," she said.

"Thank you."

We both paused, not knowing where to take it from there. She probably knew his death must be a relief to me. But of course, she couldn't say that, and neither could I. Fortunately, the phone rang, leaving her a way to end the conversation gracefully.

Choosing a shopping cart, I cruised the aisles, looking for something appealing. I passed up treats I usually bought to tempt Dad's appetite. I'd never again be able to choke down strawberry ice cream, or half a dozen other things, either.

In fact, what *did* I want to eat? The idea was confusing—not that I hadn't been buying my own food for years, but Dad had come first for so long. I'd taken care of my own basic needs, but thinking about what I wanted was a lost art.

Walking home with my bag of groceries, once again concentrating on the houses across from the school, I happened to see the roses.

Lush. Dark pink blooms, almost purplish. Every one a perfect form. The bush was tall and strong, weighted with its burden of flowers, like a miniature Atlas holding up a world.

I set my grocery bag on the sidewalk and stared. Memorizing each curled petal, each shiny leaf.

"Like my flowers?"

I looked up guiltily. I hadn't trespassed into the yard, but I felt like I'd intruded with my eyes. But the elderly woman on the porch didn't seem to mind.

"Oh," I said awkwardly, "they're beautiful."

"I started those from cuttings," she said. "Took a pair of pruning shears down to the spillway once, when my hubby was juggin' for catfish."

I assumed that was some sort of fishing. A side issue.

"Do you know what kind of roses they are?" I asked.

It was an idiotic question. How could she know? But if it seemed stupid to her, she didn't let on.

"No," she said. "I'm lucky at growing plants, but I don't know a whole lot, really. You live around here? If you want, I'll make cuttings for you."

"Oh, *would* you? I live a few blocks from here. In my dad's old house. I was taking care of him till he passed away."

"Did I know him?" she asked. "What was his name?"

"Carl Jenkins," I said. "I doubt you knew him. He wasn't all that sociable."

"Your mom was Lucille Jenkins? I knew her to speak to. Haven't seen her in a while. Is she gone, too?"

"Yes, she had a heart attack a few years ago. That's when we found out Dad had Alzheimer's. She'd been hiding it from us."

"Well, now, that's too bad. Why don't you come on in? I was about to put on the coffee—again." She laughed. "I do like my coffee, and that's the truth. Come on back to my kitchen and tell me about it."

3

I followed her through the screen door into a dark, shiny living room, and through that to a kitchen like a picture from a 1950s magazine. She pulled a chair out from her kitchen table for me and busied herself with the coffeepot for a minute or two.

"Now, I never even told you my name," she said, turning to me. "That's what Al—my hubby—says. He says, 'Mary, if you never so much as introduce yourself, how are people going to know you're not one of the bad guys?' So—I'm Mary Anderson."

"I'm Juanita Jenkins," I said. "I'm the second daughter in the family. Did we meet when I was a child? I don't remember."

"I didn't know your mom well, only to speak to. Like at the market or the post office. Or just walking past here, same as you today."

"She didn't drive," I said.

"Well, that explains it. I don't remember her with children. Maybe she did errands while you were at school?"

"Probably. What did your husband mean about being one of the bad guys?"

She smiled. "That was his little joke, on account of me being shy."

She didn't seem a bit shy to me. Maybe the joke went back to earlier years, the way jokes between married couples could do.

"So now your dad's gone, rest his soul. Are you going to move now? I could make that cutting now, set it up for you to take with, if that would be better."

"No, I'm staying," I said. "I inherited the house."

"Well, that's great. I'll set you a few extra cuttings, in case one doesn't take. You can never have too many roses, right?"

"Thank you," I said. "That's very kind."

She set cups and saucers on the table. As the coffeepot gurgled to a stop, she lifted it to pour.

"Do you take cream or sugar?"

"No, black is fine."

The cups were thick pottery, decorated with a sheaf of wheat. I knew the pattern. Around 1960, it had been a bonus in boxes of detergent. Mom had gotten them, too, but she hadn't kept them.

The memory put a lump in my throat. Not wanting to get teary in Mary's kitchen, I sipped the coffee. Dark, laced with chicory, not my favorite. But it was delicious anyway, because it was a friendship offering from a neighbor.

"Thank you," I said. "It's wonderful coffee."

"We like French Market Coffee," she said. "I used to brew it in my grandma's old biggin, but this Mr. Coffee is a lot easier. Al says it's not as good, but catch him standing over the stove, dribbling water into a biggin by spoonfuls!"

"I know what you mean," I said vaguely.

"You married? I noticed you still have your dad's name."

"No," I said. "Not married."

She smiled. "Well, it's the way for some, not for others. I guess you've had your hands full, taking care of your father. So you're staying in the old neighborhood? That'll be nice."

I looked around her kitchen, at the sun coming in through the starched curtains. The counters, clean and mostly bare, waiting for her to cook something. Everything gleaming. Perfect as a dollhouse. Not a ghost in sight.

"I have to do some remodeling," I said. "I wish my kitchen was like yours. I don't know. What with Dad's illness, somehow, it's like the house is sick, too. I don't know how to fix a place up like that, really. I've always lived in apartments."

"You'll make it your own," she said. "Of course your house isn't the way you want just yet. With your dad so sick and all? No way it could be. Have you thought about what you'd like to do?"

"For now, there's a lot of cleaning to do and junk to remove," I said. "It seems endless. The house is tired. I'm tired. I don't know where to start to make it feel right."

"It takes time," Mary said. "I remember when Al's mother passed—we had to fix up her house to sell, and it was just the saddest place. Almost like she was watching us throw out her stuff. Don't push yourself. Take a break now and then and come over for coffee. And in the spring, you'll have those roses."

Walking home, I thought about old-fashioned Southern friendliness. Maybe I could do this. Maybe I could make a place for myself here.

4

When I got home, I called the rental company to pick up the hospital bed the following day. Took out the kitchen garbage. And then I took a deep breath and went after some of the junk.

Overwhelming as it was, there might have been more. After Mom's funeral, Dad threw away everything in the attic. I'd gotten a bitter email from Manda about it.

———

Date: January 15, 2000 9:07 AM
To: Juanita Jenkins
From: Amanda Lowe
Subject: Dad

I cannot believe what Dad did. I. Can. Not. Believe. It. He threw away the Christmas decorations! Junked them! No warning, no, not him! He trashed every last hint of Christmas—the snowmen, the reindeer, the treetop angel. Mom's Christmas village, the coffee and teapot ornaments, the glass pinecones and birds, the elves—everything! Even the manger scene.

Down the deep hole at the dump, Baby Jesus!
Lots of other things, too. Our baby clothes, our
puppets, our stuffed animals! All our books!!!
Can't imagine why he stopped short of burning
the house down with everything in it!

Love,
Manda

————

Date: January 18, 2000 2:34 PM
To: Juanita Jenkins
From: Louis J. Jenkins
Subject: Fwd: Dad

Would you go and see what Dad's up to?
Manda says he's done a purge of the house.
I'm wondering if he has another woman or
something. Do you think he's planning to marry
again? Go check up, would you? We must
have some rights in this.

————

Lou dismissed the whole problem, once he satisfied
himself that a second marriage wasn't in the works.

Manda still minded, especially about the books. Since then, used copies of the books we'd loved as kids had been my typical gifts to her, and the ones she cherished. I could think of no way to replace most of the other treasures.

Not long after Manda told me that, I moved in with Dad. The comment about burning the house down had been a high-flying red flag. Because my job was at a rest home—mostly as a caregiver for people with dementia—it was a horribly familiar picture.

Not that Alzheimer's has a pattern. Everything varies from one person to another, but you get a feel for it, and destroying a family's past without a word of warning to anyone gave me that feeling.

I took time off work, visited, and saw what there was to see. It wasn't good, so I arranged to stay. Manda was astonished. I hadn't spoken to Dad in several decades, and no one had guilt-tripped me into taking care of him.

"Why, Nita?" she'd asked.

"I'm the one who knows how," I said shortly. Actually, I wasn't sure why.

But that's how I became Dad's live-in caregiver. Despite our not speaking for so long, he didn't object. Maybe he felt it was right for a daughter to take her mother's place with the housekeeping and cooking.

Lou and Manda had their careers, good careers. Mine was disposable, low paid. So it made sense for me to be the one to take care of Dad. Besides, dementia was a familiar country to me. I spoke the language, knew the customs. Knew the anger, and couldn't blame anyone for it. Who wouldn't be angry?

Manda and Lou looked at it from the outside. Manda grieved over her childhood; Lou was afraid of losing his inheritance. Her past, his future.

But Dad had neither. At the end, he had no idea who Lou and Manda were. Often, he didn't know me, either. By the time he died, he'd been gone for a while.

He didn't take the mess and problems with him. Since he'd dumped all our memories as he lost his own, getting rid of possessions was at least half done. And what was left had no value for anyone. So in one way, it was easy. On the other hand, he'd hoarded an awful lot of dingy, grubby junk. It was a big job.

"Start sooner, finish sooner," I told myself, and started with the closet. Most of the clothes would do for the thrift store, but I threw all his shoes away. He'd had athlete's foot that he refused to treat. No reason to wish it on anyone else. That filled up the garbage cans, so I'd have to quit until pickup day.

Time to do something pleasant.

I went outdoors, but the backyard had its own ghosts.

A child sits on the wooden back steps, watching her father put finishing touches on a rocking horse he built for her fourth birthday. He's a young man, so young.

"Nita, I'm sorry, but this paint won't be dry enough for you and the other kids to ride your horse at your party tomorrow."

"Oh. Okay."

Good. I don't want them to ride my horse.

The ghosts dissolved. No father, no rocking horse. No daughter. Only bare, cracked concrete and grass stubble.

Before Dad lost most of his mind and then, step-by-step, his body, I'd forced his hand about money and responsibility. I'd insisted that he make me a signer on his bank accounts and give me power of attorney—threatened to walk out if he didn't. He grumbled and wept, but he knew I meant it. So I'd been able to pay for work that had to be done, like keeping the yard mowed.

I'd done nothing extra. I'd kept the place the way he would have if he were well. Except, of course, that he'd done his own work, and I hired people. But as long as he was alive, I never made changes. I might have the power to; I didn't believe I had the right.

Now I did. And the question was—how many roses could I plant? I looked around: quite a few. Maybe the real question was, how many did I want? I'd have to ask Mary how much care her roses needed. Bushes from the wilderness at the Atchafalaya Spillway might not need much. On the other hand, if they did, even one would be too many. I'd been a full-time caretaker for several decades now—first for strangers, then for Dad. More dependents weren't a welcome idea, even if they were only plants.

The rest of the day stretched in front of me. I hadn't had free time, especially in the past six months, for anything optional, not even reading a book. A glance at the newspaper while keeping one eye on Dad had been about all I'd been able to do. Now I thought: What do people do with spare time? Or, more to the point, what would *I* do? I didn't know.

Bake something for Mary? That would be fun and neighborly, but what did I have the ingredients to make? It was too hot for another trip to the store. A loaf of bread would be a good present, but I had no yeast. There was nothing like chocolate chips or nuts to put in cookies, so that was out. I could make pound cake, but I'd feel awkward, lugging a whole cake over to the house of someone I hardly knew. Cupcakes—that was better.

I hauled out one of Mom's cookbooks, found a recipe, and got happily to work. Doing things for other people might be a hard habit to break, but at least this was optional, and likely to be pleasant.

5

The kitchen was haunted by Mom, as usual. This time, she was warming a baby bottle for Lou. Behind her were Manda and I, sitting at our table in the corner.

The girls' mother says they can sit at the table in the dining room with her and their dad someday, when they're older. She made an embroidered tablecloth for the children's table.

"Pretty flowers," says Nita, stroking the embroidery. It feels special to have their own table.

Manda frowns. "When do we get to eat with Mom and Dad?"

Ignoring them, I gathered ingredients and started my baking project. Forgot the ghosts and the past, and filled the kitchen with the scent of vanilla, butter, and chocolate. When the cupcakes came out of the oven, they were perfect. I left them cooling on racks and went back out in the yard. Baking had heated the house too much for comfort.

But again, the yard had visitors.

A four-year-old girl watches her father harvesting vegetables from the garden he planted in springtime.

"Carrots," she says. She's not sure about carrots.

"They taste better than the store ones," he tells her.

The garden is against the back fence. Beyond the back fence is an unbelievable thing—a street that stops right at their backyard! How can a street come up to a back fence and stop? The girl and her sister have both asked their dad how that can be, but they don't understand what he says. Dead end? What's that?

The father stands and takes the girl's hand. They take the vegetables inside, and he washes and peels a small carrot for her at the sink. He's right—it's much sweeter than the ones from the store. She munches on it happily. He smiles at her.

Maybe I could plant a vegetable garden next spring? I'd never been able to have one before, since I'd lived in apartments. I could hire someone for the heavy work. And get a couple of books, so it wouldn't be a disaster. Or ask some of the neighbors.

Neighbors—in more than two years as Dad's caregiver, I hadn't met even one of them. Had hardly had a chance to do anything. And, in all honesty, living in a big city had gotten me out of the habit of being friendly. Before I had a chance to talk myself out of it, I went to the next-door neighbor's front door and knocked. Since it was Saturday, most likely someone would be home.

A man answered the door, a guy about my age. He looked hard at me.

"Nita," he said.

I suddenly recognized him. The boy who lived next door when I was growing up. Neighborhood hellion, our local version of Dennis the Menace. He was bald now, and much heavier, but there was still something foxlike about him. "Charlie!"

He opened the door wide. "Come on in and sit down," he said, ushering me into the living room. "My wife and I were going to drop by your place soon— didn't want to come at a bad time, you know. Great to see you! Sorry about your dad. Sandy," he called toward the kitchen. "Bring out some of that lemonade for Nita, would you?"

A bad time, like the past couple of years, when I might have used some neighborly help? I brushed the thought aside. They probably both worked, and we'd never been close. All the same, I had a sense of sharp limits that I hadn't felt with Mary.

A woman came into the living room with tall glasses on a tray.

"Hi," she said, "I'm Sandy. Charlie's other half."

"Better half," Charlie said, winking at her.

She set the tray down on the coffee table. "It is so *hot*," she said. Actually, in their house, it wasn't. It was nice here in the cool climate of Charlie and Sandy's living room.

I took a glass and tasted. Wonderful sweet-sour lemonade, not from a mix.

"It's great," I said. "Also, I love how cool it is in here. Maybe I'll get some air conditioners. Or even a system, if they can do it."

Charlie nodded. "It's worth it," he said. "Never understood why your parents didn't go for it."

"Dad didn't like it," I said.

"It does trap you indoors," Sandy said. "You get used to it, and then it seems even hotter outside. I don't think you see people much after everyone gets it. Are you back for good, or only for a while longer? We were sorry to hear about your dad."

"Thanks." I sipped the lemonade again. "I'm back for good. Never had a chance to visit neighbors while Dad was so sick. Are your parents . . . ?" I trailed off.

"They're in a retirement place up in Covington," Charlie said. "Both doing great, but they like it better up there. Lots of friends, you know, lots of things to do.

"I think you'll get a kick out of this," he went on. "Last time I was up there, my dad told me a story. Seems your uncle came to town unexpectedly one day when your folks were out. Place was locked. So he decided to shinny in a side window. Well, this must have been about 1955, you know. People weren't so worried about that kind of thing back then.

"Anyway, Dad saw him and asked what he was doing. Your uncle said it was okay, he was your father's brother-in-law. And Dad said, 'Good to meet you. Come on over and have a beer with me till he gets home. But I can't let you climb in his window while he's gone.'"

We laughed. It was a good story. But aside from the humor, it made me sad. If someone had done that anytime recently, I suppose the neighbor would have called the police. Or gone out with a shotgun himself. Things had changed so much.

"You don't happen to know about gardening, do you?" I asked. "I was wondering about having a vegetable garden next year."

"Charlie wouldn't know a vegetable if it bit him on the ankle," Sandy said.

"Wrong," he said. "Potatoes are vegetables. I never met a potato I didn't like."

They laughed again.

"But I don't know jack about gardening," he added. "I can't even get crabgrass to grow good."

"Know of anyone else in the neighborhood I could ask?"

They exchanged glances. He shrugged. "Not really. Like I said, we don't get out too much."

God, he had changed. I remembered him as a kid, red-haired, freckled, skinny. He knew more tricks on a bicycle than a circus clown. His parents took him to the emergency room on a regular basis, but even injuries never fazed him. Someone—I was sure it was him—TP'd all the nearby hedges and trees every Halloween. One time, he put a paper bag full of dog poop on a neighbor's porch, set it on fire, rang the doorbell, and ran. The neighbor saw him, and there was a big fuss.

When his dad asked Charlie why he'd done it, he didn't have a reason. All he said was, "He's a creep. He never even comes out of his house."

6

So that was two neighbors—Mary with her wide-open heart, and Charlie, who'd somehow morphed into the man he'd hassled when he was a kid.

After I went home, I spent some time wondering if the world had changed for the worse. Much better to be like older people—like Charlie's dad or Mary—than to hide in air-conditioned comfort without caring what went on next door.

On the other hand, fantasies about the good old days were probably bunk. My parents hadn't been good neighbors. Dad had worked day and night at his failing businesses—no time to keep the place up, no money to pay anyone else to do it. No time for friendships. And Mom had been aloof and critical, nothing like Mary.

Thinking about Mary reminded me to frost the cupcakes. Deciding to get on with it, I went back to the kitchen, hoping to avoid Mom this time. I lucked out. The only ghost in the kitchen today was a ghost cake.

On Manda's ninth birthday, her mother bakes a cake—not her usual birthday cake. It's from a grocery-store magazine, a "Coronation cake." It's because of Queen Elizabeth in England. The picture on the magazine cover is beautiful, with silver sugar beads on the frosting and gumdrops for jewels.

But it tastes horrible. Bland and sticky. The girls eat one piece each, but they don't want another. The parents split a piece, and neither finishes their half. The rest of the cake stays untouched on the cake plate until it dries up. The mother offers crumbs to the birds, but they don't want them. After a few days, she throws it away.

When I took the cupcake frosting ingredients from the cabinets and refrigerator, the ghost cake disappeared from the counter. I didn't check the garbage can for it, because I was pretty sure it was in there. People ghosts were bad enough, but ghost garbage was more than I was willing to deal with.

The frosting turned out lovely, almost like fudge, but soft and buttery. I spread it thickly on the cupcakes to take over to Mary's the next day. She probably went to church on Sunday morning, if her "rest his soul" comment about Dad meant anything. So I arranged the cupcakes carefully in a glass casserole dish, covered it, and stashed them in the refrigerator to keep for afternoon. I was looking forward to seeing Mary again. Maybe I could meet Al, too, on a Sunday.

With that finished, I called the thrift store to pick up the bags of clothes, but they said they came only for furniture. "I have furniture, too," I improvised.

I hadn't planned on getting rid of furniture this soon, but why not?

We made an appointment for Tuesday between eight o'clock and noon. That gave me time to get a reasonable donation together.

After I hauled the bags of clothes out to the porch, I pushed Dad's dresser to the front hallway. Also the lamp from his room, and the lounge chair he'd lived in for a few months before he had to have the hospital bed.

Lou's and Manda's old bedrooms had been locked ever since I moved back into the house. Odd, but I assumed their furniture and childhood possessions were in there, so I stayed out. Dad had never mentioned the locked rooms, and I hadn't asked. And for the last year before he died, he hadn't said a single word—I couldn't have asked him if I'd wanted. Now, I thought, I'd better take a look.

There were no keys, but each of the knobs had a small center hole to unlatch the door in an emergency. I'd never forced a lock before, but I'd read somewhere that an ice pick was all it took. But the one from the kitchen did nothing. The beam of a small flashlight showed a tiny slot inside the hole. Rummaging in Dad's toolbox, I found a screwdriver that must have been meant for eyeglasses. When I tried it on Lou's bedroom door, the mechanism clicked. Success.

I pushed the door open cautiously in case there was something fragile behind it. There wasn't. In fact, nothing was behind the door, or anywhere else in the room. No furniture, no posters on the walls, nothing of the messy boy's room I remembered. It was stripped bare, not so much as a hanger in the closet or a thumbtack on the wall. Not even a bulb in the ceiling light fixture. When I opened Manda's door, her room was the same. Not so much as a dust bunny or a cobweb in either room. Not even a ghost.

Recalling Manda's fury when Dad dumped the Christmas decorations, I emailed her and Lou, mentioning the bare rooms and asking if they wanted anything else that might still be in the house. I offered to get a camera and send them pictures. That would take care of any doubts about what I had—and didn't.

I didn't believe they'd care about any of it, but better to be on the safe side.

7

Date: October 15, 2003 12:18 PM
To: Juanita Jenkins
From: Louis J. Jenkins
Subject: Re: Empty rooms

What do you mean, my room was empty? It wasn't empty last time I saw it. I'm sorry, but this is SO suspicious. And I don't see what a photo of an empty room would prove—don't bother. I'm sure it's empty—now. But you've had two years to empty it, haven't you?

I had a lot of good things in there. My furniture, my collection of National Geographic magazines—those must have been valuable. They went back for years. I'm going to check what they were worth, and I'll expect you to repay me. I have to think for a while about what else I had. I'll get back to you and let you know the values.

————

Date: October 15, 2003 3:21 PM
To: Louis J. Jenkins
From: Juanita Jenkins
Subject: Re: Empty rooms

Lou,

I'm a professional caregiver for the elderly. You owe me one-third of the value of full-time live-in care of our father for two years, seven months, one week, and four days. Also a third of his medical and burial expenses.

Nita

PS—Back issues of National Geographic sell for a nickel apiece at the thrift store here. Let me know how many you had, and I'll deduct it from your bill.

————

It was satisfying to click the Send button on that email. Lou had always been a brat. Six years younger than I, he was a late baby. Unplanned, probably. Dad, in disconnected ramblings before his final year of muteness, had told me that Mom had accused him of browbeating her to get an abortion. It was—barely—believable, because it would explain why she'd always acted like she was defending Lou from something, like it was the two of them against the world.

But I had no way to know what had happened. Maybe she'd said that. Maybe she hadn't. Maybe he'd done that. Maybe he hadn't. And he'd said a lot of off-the-wall things as Alzheimer's closed in on him. Even though I knew his final silence was a bad sign, it came as a relief.

There were other reasons Mom might have spoiled Lou.

Two girls come to the breakfast table, but their mother isn't there. Their father offers them cereal. He says there's no time for anything else. They have to get ready—they're going to the hospital to visit their mother. She was sick in the night.

The younger girl wonders if her mother is going to die. What happens to children whose mothers die? Dads don't take care of the house and feed the children. They go to work. On weekends, they make wood things in the garage.

The hospital is strange. It smells funny. It's cold. Their father brings their mother a tin of coffee-flavored candy. She gives each girl one piece.

Their father says, "How are you feeling?"

She begins to sob. The girls have never seen their mother cry before.

"I was sure it was a boy," she says.

———

Date: October 15, 2003 11:14 PM
To: Juanita Jenkins
From: Amanda Lowe
Subject: Re: Empty rooms

Dear Nita,

I don't remember what was in my old room,
so don't worry about it. That must have been
weird. Open the door—tah dah! And then . . .
nothing. Doesn't surprise me—not after the
way he dumped our past when Mom died.
Please don't send photos of what's left of my
teenage room—I'm afraid I might get acne
again just looking at it.

You've lived in a house with two locked rooms
for a couple of years? That must have been
weird, too. Shades of Bluebeard. Sounds like
your life with Dad was weird all around. Can't
say I'm all that surprised at that, either.

You know what else is strange? No dust
bunnies? No cobwebs? If you have the secret

of a self-cleaning room there, I wish you'd let
me in on it.

Love,
Manda

———

So Manda was okay, and there was no point worry-
ing about Lou. Grabbing the dish of cupcakes from the
refrigerator at the last minute, I headed over to Mary's.

I lucked out—she was home, and so was Al. He
wasn't fazed by an unexpected visitor at the door, and
the chocolate cupcakes probably didn't hurt, either.

Mary came out of the kitchen, wiping her hands
on a flour-sack towel.

"Well, isn't that nice," she said when she saw the
cupcakes. "Let's have a cup of coffee and give these a
try. They look delicious!"

"So you're Nita," Al said, turning off the TV. "Mary
told me she'd met you. I love it when people come
back to the neighborhood—but I'm sorry about your
Dad."

"Thanks," I said.

Mary got the coffeepot going again, but Al didn't
wait for coffee before taking a cupcake.

"These are great!" he said. "Mary, you think you can talk her out of the recipe?"

I laughed. "Sure she can. If she wants it."

"Not sure you *need* all those cupcakes," Mary said.

"Oh, I do!"

She flapped her hand at him. "Go on, Al!"

I enjoyed the way they kidded each other, the way they were friends. If I'd ever gotten married, that's what I would have wanted.

She turned to me. "If you like, I could take a look at your yard and see where roses might do well. I don't want you to put them someplace they won't bloom."

Luckily, I had a piece of cupcake in my mouth, so she didn't expect a quick answer. Because it occurred to me—could anyone else see the ghosts?

8

A mother and three-year-old daughter sit together on the couch in the living room. The mother is tatting a lacy placemat for a set she's been working on for years. Her shuttle is bright steel. The room is dim, but the shuttle flashes anyway.

"If you hadn't had pneumonia when you were two, I would have finished college," she says. "I had to drop out because you were sick."

The daughter understands. Once you leave school, you're not allowed to go back. It's like magical stories where you only get three wishes. She doesn't go to school yet. Manda does. The girl is sorry she made her mother leave school.

"I'll leave you this luncheon set in my will," the mother says.

The daughter hates lace, especially tatted lace. She knows she can't say so. She knows a will is for when you die, and she doesn't want to think about her mother dying. She opens a book on her lap.

"Will you read me a story?" she asks.

"Not now."

The girl looks at the book. She knows the black squiggles are the story. She doesn't know the word "code" yet, but she intuits that she needs to break a code. Curiosity takes over her frustration. It feels exciting. She slides off the couch and takes the book to ask her sister about the squiggles. Her mother looks up briefly and goes back to her handwork.

Would Mary have seen them, if I'd brought her home to look for rose-garden locations? If not, if I were seeing things others couldn't, I was probably going crazy. True, the ghosts never spoke to me, and they always disappeared fairly quickly. I'd never heard of actual hallucinations being so accommodating.

But what if they were visible to other people? What if Mary or someone else walked in the kitchen and saw Mom lying dead on the floor? She was there often—I'd learned to step around her as I fixed meals or put away groceries. In another couple of weeks, I'd probably be walking right through her. But if anyone else saw her, they'd freak. It would certainly be the end of any friendship. They might even call the police.

And the thrift-store crew was coming on Tuesday. The rental company had picked up Dad's hospital bed without any ghosts appearing, but it might not be a good idea to push my luck. Better move my donations onto the front porch instead of letting the truck driver into the house to get them. If *he* saw a dead woman on the kitchen floor, all hell would break loose.

Better reconsider the plan to meet more neighbors and get gardening help and advice, too, at least for a while.

What *could* I do? There was no one to ask. I felt lost and clueless. Lou probably wasn't speaking to me after our email exchange, and I didn't want to confide in him, anyway. He might pretend I was incompetent so he could contest the will. Manda would be more sympathetic, but she might be worried I was losing my mind, and maybe she'd be right.

I might ask the ghosts themselves whether they were visible to anyone but me, but I doubted they'd answer. At least so far, they didn't seem to be aware of me. I could try, next time I saw one, but it didn't seem smart to pin my hopes on any information from them.

In movies, people went to priests with this kind of problem. But my experience with priests was limited to my schooling, and one of the main things I'd learned was not to trust them.

I didn't trust psychiatrists, either. Wasn't it their business for their patients to be crazy? If I went to one of them with stories about seeing ghosts, they'd have me on some magic-potion drug in no time. Forget shrinks.

But I remembered—when I worked at the rest home, my supervisor said that her grandmother's ghost would appear to her and her sister when someone in the family was about to die. At least *she* wouldn't think I was crazy if I asked.

————

Date: October 17, 2003 2:03 PM
To: Sarah Maccomber
From: Juanita Jenkins
Subject: Question

Dear Sarah,

I hope it isn't too weird to ask you about this, but I remembered you said that you and your sister had seen your grandmother's ghost walking in your house shortly before your mother passed away. Since my father died, I've been seeing ghosts in the house—not only him, but my whole family. Since my sister and brother are still alive, they're not ghosts exactly. I don't know what to call them.

I see incidents in our lives like scenes from plays. Sometimes the ghosts talk to one another, but they never seem to notice me.

I know it sounds crazy, but I don't think I'm
losing my mind. I'm taking care of things, and
I don't feel upset or depressed. I've decided
to stay here, and I'm making friends in the
neighborhood. Spending my days sorting
and disposing of my dad's junk, and deciding
ordinary things like whether to have air
conditioning installed.

Can you shed any light on this? You're the only
person I could think to ask.

Nita Jenkins

———

I clicked Send, wondering if she'd even answer. Or
if she'd know. I'd tried to find halfway credible information about ghosts on the Internet, but most of what
I'd come up with was stories similar to hers—visions
of family members that preceded a death.

Other stories on the Internet sounded like complete
bullshit to me. But maybe the reason they weren't believable was that they hadn't been told to me by a person
I knew, someone who didn't fall for every dumb fad
that came along.

So what if Sarah didn't answer me? Friends and relatives
were out, priests and therapists were out. What was left?

What about the library? I'd been planning to go there anyway to check out some gardening books. And it was mid-October, the perfect time to look up information about ghosts without seeming completely loony. I could make something up for the librarians—say I was having a party, and wanted some believable ghost stories to tell. They'd probably be glad to help.

9

It took some heavy pushing and lifting, but I manhandled the furniture onto the porch Tuesday morning. I put a sign on it that said "thrift-store donation." I decided to go to the hardware store later and buy a dolly or at least some furniture sliders. There was a lot more furniture to get rid of, and I'd hurt my back if I kept doing it the hard way.

And then I left for the library. The neighborhood branch was still in the old location, but it wasn't open yet. I walked around the shopping center—or mini-mall, or whatever it was called now. Almost all the stores I remembered were gone.

Some changes were for the better. Across the street had been a "private club" with a swimming pool. Except, if you were white, it *wasn't* private. You paid 75 cents to buy a "membership" for the day.

We didn't understand what that meant. To us, it was only a swimming pool. We went there in summer as often as we could. The "club" had shut down when Jim Crow segregation became illegal. Now an office building stood on the site.

In spite of vivid memories of the shopping center, I didn't see a single ghost. Apparently, they could only appear in my own house and yard. That was encouraging—made me feel that perhaps I wasn't hallucinating, anyway. But if the ghosts weren't hallucinations, what could they be?

When it was opening time for the library, I headed over there. Inside, it was cool, and the fluorescent lights gave the room a greenish cast, exactly as I remembered.

For a second, it was like going back in time, back to a vivid memory of finding a wonderful book about an Appaloosa horse named Frosty Morning—it had been in the left-hand corner near the floor. I half expected to see an eight-year-old, horse-crazy Nita browsing the stacks.

But the children's books were gone from that bookcase, and my ghost wasn't there, either. There was no one else in the room but the librarian.

"Can I help you?" she asked.

"I'm looking for books on gardening and ghosts."

She smiled. "Together, or separately?"

"Now that would be a specialty," I mused. "Gardening ghosts. No, sorry—I was slightly incoherent there. I meant, I'm looking for books on gardening and more or less factual information about ghosts, if such a thing exists."

"Factual?"

"Well, documented, anyway. Not 'The Legend of Sleepy Hollow.' I'm trying to write a believable ghost story for a Halloween party."

"Paranormal research, then," she said. She turned to her computer and tapped keys for a few seconds.

"You'll find that on the shelves in the 130s," she told me. She tapped a bit more. "Also, there's a lot on the Internet. Much of it's crackpot—some of them are even selling 'ghost-hunting kits,' so *caveat emptor*. If it's for a party, I don't suppose it would be important if it's baloney, as long as it's semi-credible baloney." Looking up, she added, "Gardening's in the 635 section."

"Thanks. How do I get a library card, by the way?"

"Bring in ID with your name and address. One official photo ID or two of something else, like utility bills or recent letters."

I thought about that. "I've been a caregiver for my father for the past couple of years. I don't have anything."

"No driver's license?"

"I don't drive."

"Not even a state ID card?"

"I never needed one."

"What about bills? Everyone has bills."

"All the accounts are in my dad's name. I haven't changed it since he passed away."

"Oh, I'm sorry," she said. It came out like she thought it was her fault, but I was sure she didn't mean it that way.

Best to change the subject. "Maybe my address is on his will. I don't remember."

"Well, that would be one. Do you have a voter registration card?"

"I never voted in Louisiana."

She looked more intrigued than annoyed, as if this were a choice research problem.

"Letters?"

"I have a letter from Dad's lawyer. But it's part of the whole package with the will."

"Any other mail?"

"I don't think so. I generally use email. Even the junk mail is addressed to Dad, or Resident."

"Well, I might stretch a point and call the will and the letter two IDs. Especially if you have the envelope. But see if you can find something else, okay?"

"I have a power of attorney. My address may be on the paper—maybe not. Or, what I mean is, it might not be clear it was my address if it does have one. I was living in Dad's house. There might be other things. I'll look. Meantime, I'll sit and read awhile in here."

"That'll be fine. Let me know if you need any more help." She gave me another smile before turning back to the computer.

I found the sections she'd mentioned—lots about gardening, all of it looking authoritative. I could come back for one or two of these when I got my library card.

The paranormal section was a mixed bag. Psychic phenomena of all kinds were covered. At least the authors were taken seriously enough to have been published. They hadn't just been dismissed as nutcases. On the other hand, there were so many different kinds of experience, from reincarnation to varying versions of heaven and hell.

I took several of the books to a table to see if I could get some general ideas about the ghosts. As I was paging through them, it occurred to me that, with almost no formal identity, I was not far from being a sort of ghost myself.

10

After I'd been puzzling over the paranormal books for half an hour or so, the librarian came to my table.

"Are you finding what you want?" she asked. "It's a fairly large subject."

"I thought I'd read something about ghosts that reenacted past events. I was sort of moving in that direction for my story, but I haven't found anything."

"Ah," she said. "The Akashic Records."

"What's that?" I asked. Obviously not the type of record that could get you a library card.

"It's a sort of book of life," she said. "A recording in energy of everything that's ever been felt, said, or done."

She went to a shelf and fetched a book for me. "It's an intriguing subject," she said. Noticing a patron approaching her desk, she went to see what he wanted.

The book she'd chosen was about Edgar Cayce. He had a lot to say about these Akashic Records. It wasn't that readable, but I skimmed through it, picking up ideas. The records themselves appeared to be a complete history of everything, and the purpose was individual growth and transformation. A lot of the book was case histories of psychic readings—not especially interesting to me.

There wasn't anything about actually reliving experiences like watching a play—it seemed to be more like reading books about the past. Still, it was good to know that other people had thought about things like this.

I reshelved the books, gave the librarian a friendly wave, and left. When I got home, the thrift-store donation was gone, replaced with a generic sort of receipt for my taxes. I took it inside.

In the foyer, a girl silently watches her father holding her new baby brother in the living room. "My son, my son," the father croons. He doesn't notice his daughter a few steps away. She's baffled by her father's words. Yes, the baby is his son. But . . . so?

Walking past them as if they were manikins, I went to my desk and turned on the computer. I'd thought of looking for more information on Akashic Records, but first I checked my email.

––––––––––

Date: October 18, 2003 4:24 PM
To: Juanita Jenkins
From: Sarah Maccomber
Subject: Re: Question

Nita,

I'm sorry to hear about your father. I hope his passing was peaceful.

If you're seeing earlier images of people who are still alive, as well as those who have passed on, they're visions, not ghosts. I suppose they could be produced by powerful memories, and I'd think their presence is supposed to complete your understanding of some issue that's been on your mind. Once you've resolved what's troubling you, I think the visions will disappear, so please don't worry, but try to learn what you can.

You've had an incredibly stressful few years. I know you're a professional caregiver, but it's different when it's your own parent. It was right for you to help your dad as he struggled with dementia, but it had to be painful, and your mom died shortly before that. It's hardly surprising that your mind is choosing an unusual way of dealing with the experience.

Please let me know how it all works out. I'll be glad to discuss it with you more, if you'd like.

Sarah

———

Date: October 18, 2003 6:10 PM
To: Juanita Jenkins
From: Louis J. Jenkins
Subject: Re: Empty rooms

You've always been a royal pain. No wonder
no one likes you.

Lou

———

Lou's blast was nothing new, but its sting was surprising. He had standard gibes, and that was one of
his favorites. I had my scripted comebacks, too. This
time, I decided not to use any of them. If, as Sarah
said, this was a time for reevaluating and resolving old
issues, step one might be refusing to fight old fights
for the thousandth time. I deleted Lou's email without
answering, and wrote a brief thank-you to Sarah.

I thought about the practical things I wanted to do,
and realized that most of them would involve letting
people into the house. That had already occurred to me
about gardening, but it didn't stop there. Getting air conditioning was out, for sure. And getting the car fixed—

a mechanic or a tow-truck guy would have to pick it up, and that would mean going in the backyard, at least. I could go out to a driving school for lessons—they'd have their own cars—but there didn't seem much point until I had a usable car of my own. Would they see the ghosts? Probably not—but I couldn't be sure.

No, if the purpose of the ghosts, or visions, or whatever they were was for me to learn something, I should pay close attention. I decided to take notes about their appearances and see what I could make of them. Seemed the only way I'd ever get back to a normal life.

11

I found a notebook and started a record of the ghosts' appearances. It occurred to me—why hadn't Dad stripped my room as he had Lou's and Manda's? Also, when had he destroyed theirs? Was it right after Mom's funeral, during the time when he'd dumped all the Christmas ornaments and childhood treasures? And one more question—why?

Or had he done it at all? Maybe it was Mom. But again, when and why?

When I'd moved in with Dad nearly three years ago, my room looked nearly undisturbed. It had been straightened, but my furniture was still there, still in the same arrangement. And in all the time since, I'd done little more than unpack my clothes and put them away. I hadn't had time or attention for the boxes of possessions on the closet shelves and floor.

Opening one now, I found my plush kangaroo, a few books, and the nautilus shell I'd kept on my dresser for years, along with its wire stand, now tarnished and bent. One of the books was a library book, several decades overdue. In fact, it was the horse book I'd remembered so vividly the day I visited the library. I didn't remember swiping it deliberately, but there it was.

Obviously, I'd have to take it back. I could only imagine what fine they'd charge for nearly half a century. Maybe they had a wholesale rate, like per decade instead of per day? I remembered one library that didn't charge more in fines than the value of the book. But what value? When it was published, or its current value, which might be considerable?

I straightened the shell's stand and set it up on the dresser where it had been for so many years. Beside it, I propped the plush kangaroo.

And then I sat down with the notebook. It was hard to remember the visions in order, but I did my best. They made no sense that way. I took a fresh page, and tried to rearrange them as the events had happened. After half an hour of mulling it over, erasing, and rewriting, I still didn't get it. Even setting aside my imagined reconstruction of Mom's death, which was out of chronological order, I didn't see much of a pattern.

I tried adding the memories that had struck me since Dad's death:

Ghosts

Mom dead on the floor (numerous times)

Mom preparing food in the kitchen (numerous times)

Dad's garden

Manda and I eating in the kitchen while our parents ate in the dining room

Teaching myself to read

The rocking horse

Being dropped off at school to fend for myself

Wondering why Mom hadn't been proclaimed Miss America

The Coronation cake

Mom giving up on her college degree (and blaming me for getting pneumonia)

Mom's miscarriage

Possibility that Dad wanted Mom to abort Lou

Dad's delight that Lou was a boy

A vague pattern—two people trying to make it as parents. Mostly enjoying their children, at least for a few years. But more and more, they realized they'd gotten in over their heads. Then a surprise third child—the previously much-longed-for son.

And then what? Why would getting what you want most be the very thing that would make your life come apart?

Baffled, I decided to take a break. I laid the library book on the hall table so I wouldn't forget to take it there with me next time. I stacked the other books with it—might as well give them to the library, if they wanted them.

And then I turned back to the living room.

A nine-year-old girl approaches her father, who is reading a magazine.

"Dad," she says. "My shoes are way too small, and they're falling apart. I need some new ones."

He looks up. "Don't worry, honey. We'll take care of you."

"But Dad," she persists, "I only have this one pair. So I need new ones."

"Not now," he says. "I can't afford it." He goes back to his magazine.

The girl goes to her sister and explains the problem. An hour later, her sister quietly gives her a twenty-dollar bill.

"For your shoes," she says. "We'll go to the shopping center together this weekend."

"How did you do it?" the girl asks.

"You have to know how to ask."

She could see that Manda knew how to ask. Was know-ing how to ask the big secret? Was it something you were born with? If you were one of the unlucky ones who didn't know, did that mean you'd never get what you want?

12

The next morning, I was standing outside the library when it opened. I half-hoped another librarian would be on duty, but it was the woman who'd helped me before.

"Hi," she said brightly. "Did you bring your ID?"

"Yes." I waited for her to turn on the lights, lock her purse in her desk drawer, and power up her computer.

When she was settled, she turned to me expectantly. But instead of giving her documents, I fished the horse book out of my bag.

"This was in a box at home," I said. "It seems to be . . . rather dramatically overdue." I stopped, embarrassed. Any excuse would sound ridiculously lame.

She opened it to the back and examined the check-out card. A smile twitched at the corners of her lips.

"Looks that way," she agreed.

"I'm not sure what happened," I said. "I suspect I snitched it. I don't remember doing it, but I did love the book."

"And how old were you?"

"Eight."

"Ah. Well, you'd hardly fit in with the population of Juvenile Hall at this point. Why don't we accept it as a gift from time?" She smiled a full smile this time, and laid the book on a table by her desk.

"Don't I owe a fine?"

"Not on a gift from time," she said. "Seriously, don't worry about it. We encourage people to bring back books that have been out a long time. Some libraries even have an amnesty day once a year, and I've been encouraging Jefferson Parish to do it."

"Thanks." I took the other books out of my bag. "These were in the same box. They were mine when I was a child. They seem like nice books. Can you use them?"

She looked them over. "Do you know this *Arabian Nights* is a rare book? It's a first edition, and the illustrations are by Edmund Dulac."

I shrugged. "I don't want to keep it, and I'm not interested in selling it."

"I can't shelve an antiquarian book," she said. "If I accept it, it would be to sell. The money would go into our acquisition fund. But it's valuable—are you sure you want to donate it?"

"Yes," I said. "Think of it as a gift from time."

I peeked at the name sign on her desk and asked, "You're Enid Stone?" It sounded stupid, but sometimes people sit at other people's desks.

"C'est moi." She always seemed on the verge of a smile, as if whatever a person told her was what she'd always wanted to hear.

"I'm Nita Jenkins," I said. "Juanita is my whole name, but I go by Nita."

"Juanita's such a pretty name," she said.

I didn't tell her it came with baggage. Other people's baggage about foreign names. Instead, I said, "So's Enid. Reminds me of Enid Bagnold."

Another smile. "You really did like horse books, didn't you?"

"Yes. It's funny, when I finally got close to a real horse, I was afraid of it. But the books are still great memories."

"One of the many advantages of reading," she agreed. "You can be an armchair traveler—or an armchair equestrienne."

"Or even an armchair horse."

"*That's* quite an image. By the way, how are you doing with your ghost story?"

"Bewildered, to put it mildly. Every writer is sure they have the truth, the whole truth, and nothing but the truth. But they disagree completely."

"Hmmm . . . lots of subjectivity there. But if you're writing a story, what difference would it make? Pick the approach you like, and go with it."

"Well," I said uncomfortably, "It isn't actually for a story." It wasn't often I had to confess to both theft and lying in the course of one conversation. But Enid didn't look at all upset.

"Oh, really?" she said. "Tell."

"Long story," I said. "Maybe we could have lunch together sometime?"

"A weekend would be best. I bring a sack lunch here. But I don't work Saturday or Sunday. You live around here, right?"

"Right," I said. "I even brought proof of address." I fished in the bag again.

We went through the library card application, which was short. "Are you in the neighborhood, too?" I asked, as she handed me the card.

"Just around the corner. If you'd like, we could grab lunch somewhere around here next Saturday."

13

On the way home, I thought happily about how much easier it had been for me to meet people here—California had always seemed so unfriendly. Maybe it was southern friendliness. Maybe being a middle-aged woman was a plus—it might be harder for a man to be accepted so quickly, at least with women. I didn't know. Other than work, I hadn't had any connections with men for a long time. Whatever the reason, it was wonderful to feel liked.

I breezed into the house and nearly ran into Mom and Dad in the living room, obviously in the middle of a serious quarrel.

"If you hadn't quit your job the day Lou was born, I wouldn't be taking all these calls from bill collectors," the mother says.

"Why don't you help instead of always criticizing?"

"Going into business for yourself—I had a baby, so you had to have one, too."

"And you're keeping him a baby, aren't you? My son, the mama's boy."

"Lou is the only one who's mine—you took the girls away from me."

"I never took anyone away from you. But you don't give a damn about anyone but Lou anymore!"

"I wish I'd never had children!"

"For God's sake, don't say that where they can hear you."

I looked at them blankly. They faded, then reappeared in the dining room, repeating their conversation like a recording. Then in the kitchen. Then in another place in the living room. Then everywhere at once. Their voices blended in a cacophony of fury.

I backed into the entry hall and fumbled briefly before my fingers mastered the trick of turning the doorknob behind me. Finally releasing the catch, I slipped out onto the porch and closed the door softly. After a slow count of ten, I went cautiously back inside. They were gone.

I'd probably never witnessed that quarrel as a single scene—it was a collection of bitter gibes over the years, a never-ending drama. Maybe that was why I'd seen them all over the house this time. Every one of those lines was an old, old story.

And each of my parents had had a point—Dad *had* been irresponsible to quit his job with a new baby in the house, not to mention the two children already there. And it hadn't been a single business venture, either. That one had failed, and the next, and the next. I'd counted once—there'd been seven bankrupt businesses in the years between Lou's birth and the day I walked out with nothing but Dad's old army rucksack on my back and my piggybank money in my pocket.

And Mom *had* been all but insane about Lou. Physically, he did what infants do—grow up. But he never stopped being her baby. She cut up his food, spooned the sugar into his tea, waited on him while she ignored everyone else.

She'd been on his side, no matter what he did. When I was fifteen years old and he was nine, I'd woken to find him in my bedroom, lifting my nightgown and peering underneath. Even that was fine, according to Mom.

She'd literally still been wiping his butt for him when he was ten years old. Manda was away at college by then, and Dad was working about twenty hours a day at another failing business. My home had turned into a small, private madhouse, and I mostly stayed in my room with the door closed. Or stayed away altogether.

In those years, the thought of a normal family was like a vision of heaven. The things other people took for granted, I could only imagine—comfort, security, cleanliness. Most of all, love. I was so vulnerable, I didn't have an Achilles *heel*— I had a whole Achilles body.

14

On Saturday, Enid picked me up in front of the library. As soon as I was settled in the passenger seat of her car, she suggested a local sandwich place for lunch.

"Not just because it's close," she explained. "They make a great oyster po' boy."

"Sounds great."

As she turned onto Metairie Road, she asked, "How did it happen that you never learned to drive?" She was giving her attention to traffic, and I was reluctant to distract her with an answer. But as I hesitated, she looked toward me, and that was worse, so I went ahead.

"I guess it sort of developed. I have Dad's car now, but no one has driven it in years, and I'd need to have a mechanic check it out. And I'd have to take driving lessons, but it's not practical yet."

She turned onto a side street and parked the car. As we got out, she asked, "Why not? I mean, if you don't mind my asking."

"It has to do with ghosts," I said awkwardly.

At the restaurant, we found a corner table a little away from other patrons. When we'd ordered, she sipped her ice water. "Tell me more," she said.

"I've been seeing ghosts in the house," I said. "Or maybe they're not ghosts. A friend of mine calls them visions."

A bad start. I tried again.

"I think I told you I'd been a caregiver for my father? Well, he was living in the house I grew up in, and now it's mine. But I keep seeing him—and my mom, and my sister and brother, and me—all over the house."

"Really? What are these visions about?"

"Scenes from the past. I suppose it sounds crazy."

"Not at all. You said your dad passed away recently? What about your mom?"

"She died a few years ago. Suddenly. That's when we found out Dad had Alzheimer's."

"So you were his caregiver after that. Are your brother and sister still living?"

"Yes. I'm closer to my sis than to my brother."

"My guess is the 'ghosts' are leftover emotional energy from intense experiences in the house. I gather they're not doing everyday tasks like peeling apples and mopping floors."

"Mostly not. But even the everyday, normal things they do feel intense."

She nodded. "I can see why. What else did your friend say? The one who called them visions."

"That it was a form of teaching. That they'd go away once I learned what I needed to."

"I agree. But what's the connection with driving lessons?"

"I'm afraid other people will see them. If someone came to the house, or even into the yard, they might be there."

I took a bite of my sandwich. It was good, with a crisp crust over creamy oysters, stuffed into a half loaf of French bread. Enid ate a few bites of hers, considering what I'd told her.

Finally, she said, "I doubt other people could see them. On the other hand, if *you* saw one while someone was in your house, you'd probably seem strained and tense. Maybe it's a good idea to wait a while, but it's also probably good to go out often, so you don't feel isolated and get obsessed."

"That sounds reasonable," I said.

"You might think of your house as a sort of school," she went on. "It has a lot to offer you right now, but it can't be your whole life."

During the rest of the meal, conversation veered to other topics: her job at the library, my job in California, typical getting-acquainted chitchat. We finished our sandwiches, paid, and left.

She dropped me off at home, and I drew a deep breath on the front porch, hoping the house wouldn't be full of quarreling. At least the deep breath prepared me for something else.

An eleven-year-old girl stands on the front porch of her home. With the door still closed, she can smell inside.

Her mother has cats, many cats. They do not go outdoors. They have no litter box. When the cats soil the floor, the mother lays a sheet of newspaper over the mess. After five or six of these layers have piled up, she stuffs them in the garbage and starts over.

The girl has never known another house that reeked before she even opened the door. Even when she was younger, she rarely invited friends over. Now she never does.

I opened the door. There they were, Mom's matted, bedraggled silver-tipped Persian cats. They glared languidly and stupidly in my direction. The smell was overpowering. And sure enough, when I checked the usual corner of the kitchen, there were the foul newspapers, probably at least four layers of them. It all faded slowly and then disappeared, cats, papers, and poops. Even the smell was gone.

And then an odd thought hit me: If I could only get a patent on cats with disappearing poop, I could make a fortune. Ghost cat shit came close to being the funniest thing I had ever heard of. Standing in that empty kitchen, I laughed and laughed at what was no longer there.

15

After the ghost cats, I saw quick flashes of other pets. My kitten that died when I was four years old for lack of a cheap, routine shot. My dog that Mom gave away when Lou was born, "in case she bites the baby." Lou's purebred tricolor collie, which became mine when he wouldn't take care of her. And a fleeting picture of the way Lou had gloated when the collie, too, had died because she hadn't had vaccinations.

Besides seeing more and more ghosts, I started drawing, more or less out of the blue. I'd never had any artistic talent before. But suddenly, my hands would move almost by themselves, pick up any pen or pencil that was lying around, grab a scrap of paper, and draw. They were good drawings, too—far beyond just recognizable. They were accomplished. And they were always drawings of good memories.

One was the night Dad took me to a ballet. He was so tired, he'd fallen asleep in his seat. But he'd taken me anyway. His sleeping face in the dimness of the theater was shown at one side of the picture, with the dancers pirouetting in the far background, a study in contrast.

Another was Mom at her sewing machine, making Halloween costumes for Manda and me.

Day after day, the drawings jumped into life: Birthday parties. Homework help. A doll chewed by Charlie's dog, taken to work by Dad for repair by an artist there. The baby mockingbird we'd fostered until it was ready to fly on its own. A trip to Ship Island. Going to the zoo at Audubon Park and watching the seals being fed. Hiding candies and dyed eggs in the yard for Lou, early on Easter morning. Dad making French toast for Sunday breakfast. Reading us stories at bedtime, making hand shadows on the wall. Mom in culottes, turning cartwheels in the backyard.

The pictures were of happy times, but to me, they were saddest of all. Our troubles had been an avalanche that swept it all away. Swept me away, too—I'd never come back. Not until Mom died on the kitchen floor and Dad was so sick he barely recognized me. As I finished each drawing, I sobbed bitterly over it. Even though I knew there was nothing a child could have done to change what happened, I blamed myself for everything I'd lost.

I tried to crumple one drawing and throw it away, but the next day, it lay smoothly on the dining room table. Pencils and paper appeared all over the house, and without warning, I might find myself drawing another picture. Mom finding four-leaf clovers, which she had a genius for spotting. Or Manda and I sneaking out to a lovely wooded area we found, supposedly off-limits because we had to cross a neighbor's land to get there. Days at Pontchartrain Beach—the carousel, cotton candy, swimming—and in the evenings there, free clown and acrobat shows.

Somehow, none of the good times had mattered. The candy had dissolved the way cotton candy always does, but so had every good thing that ever happened. I wondered why.

And I also began to wonder: Was my family that unusual? I knew a few neighborhood secrets—how Charlie's mother had spent time in rehab for alcoholism, and a man down the street had gone to prison for some financial fiddle. And sometimes, children know more than they understand—as an adult, I realized that one of my childhood friends had probably been molested by her father. Another had died of meningitis; another had been crippled by polio, even though the shots were available. Had I really had it that bad?

———

Date: November 1, 2003 12:21 AM
To: Louis J. Jenkins
From: Juanita Jenkins
Subject: Pax

Lou,

We didn't get along well when we were children. But we haven't seen each other in decades. What if we were to start new rap sheets for each other? You never know, we might turn out to be friends.

Nita

———

It was one thing to decide to go for walks, look around the neighborhood, and get out of the house. Another to do it, push myself out into cold or rainy weather. And November could be cold and rainy in New Orleans, regardless of its reputation as a tropical paradise. I caught a bus downtown to shop for sweaters and a warm coat, so cold days wouldn't keep me indoors.

I'd ridden buses all over the city when I was in high school. I'd refused to go back to the horrible religious school after ninth grade. I probably got away with it because Dad was having trouble affording it anyway. The public school I should have attended was so rough, it was out of the question. So I sneaked into one that wasn't in my district.

When I transferred, I lied about my address, my phone number, and almost everything else except my name. Of course, they caught on after a while. But the principal wasn't eager to kick me out—I made straight As and never broke a rule, so he was content to let me know he knew. With over a thousand kids in the school, a good student who didn't belong there was the least of his worries.

Every morning, I commuted into Uptown New Orleans, sharing buses with office workers, domestics, and assorted cranks. Before 1956, when buses were desegregated, a movable sign had separated them into two sections—white and "colored." By the time I was in high school, the signs had been removed. Refusing to accept informal segregation, blacks sat wherever they liked, often one person to a double seat. Usually, whites stood, clutching the overhead rails as if the bus were full. At first, I did what was expected of me and stood, too. And then I got sick of it, sick of the stupid hatred, and sat in any available seat. In time, everyone would do this. In the short run, I reaped a lot of hate-filled stares.

Instead of going home in the afternoons, I prowled the city on more buses or on foot, often not returning till late at night. Mom and Dad never objected. By then they'd given up on me, or maybe they'd given up on everything. The racial hatred on the buses was trivial compared to the loathing that lay in our house like ground fog. I counted the days until I was old enough to leave forever.

At first, my struggles for freedom led me in a positive direction. My schoolmates were much nicer than the private school kids had been, and I made friends.

Socially, the public high school was divided about in half—a mixture of college-bound kids from the University District and working-class kids from the area around Magazine Street, including its housing projects. In school jargon, the "frats" and the "cats." Though all were white—school desegregation had indeed begun, as my parents had feared, but it was going slowly, one grade at a time—other cultural divides played a part. Money, of course. Also, the "frats" were largely Jewish and the "cats" were Irish and Italian Catholics.

I didn't fit with either group, though I had friends on both sides. I was Episcopal, beat out most of the frats academically, and spoke like them. Socially, I had more in common with the cat girls. I liked their outspokenness, and of course, with as little money as I had for clothes and haircuts, I resembled them more than I did the sleek frats.

I might have belonged solidly to either group if I'd tried. But it was a drawback that I didn't live in the district—I couldn't invite friends home. And I had no knack for belonging. No longer a pariah, I was still an outsider.

If I'd melded with the cat group, my life might have turned out like Mary's—a comfortable marriage with a blue-collar guy, being a stay-at-home mom for one or two kids, a decent retirement, roses in the front yard. Or if I'd thrown in with the frats, I might have been more like Enid—single, college-educated for a good job in library science or teaching, independent, free to do what I wanted. Either way might have been a good life. But that wasn't how it worked out.

16

My shopping trip to Canal Street was puzzling. Of course, I'd expected change, but I wasn't prepared for so much. During my high school years, I'd drifted through the big department stores often, putting off going home in the afternoons. I could rarely buy anything—I barely had money for bus fare home. But I could look at the things other people could have, and I could dream. The stores were fresh with air conditioning, and the cosmetic counters were redolent with expensive perfume. Mirrors, marble, the scent of new fabrics—perfection everywhere.

And when I passed through the door labeled "White Women," I found more mirrors, gleaming stainless steel and porcelain fixtures, immaculate tile. Sometimes there was an attendant offering hand towels, but that was embarrassing, since I couldn't afford to tip. In my naiveté, I assumed that identical facilities lay behind the "Colored Women" door.

Now, everything was different. Of course, I knew the Jim Crow signs would be gone, and was glad of it. But the department stores were gone, too. Their buildings had been converted to hotels and restaurants.

I finally found a shopping mall called Canal Place and bought what I needed, but nothing more. It had been a long time since I cared how I looked, and even with money, I couldn't bring back the wistful yearning for nice things that had brought me to town when I was young. It was strange to be able to afford anything and to want so little.

Leaving the mall, I walked up Canal Street, remembering some blocks vividly, trying to decipher others. I recalled childhood trips to gaze at the animated Christmas displays in the windows of the Holmes and Maison Blanche stores—surely Dad must have brought us, since we weren't old enough to go by ourselves. Surely he'd stood with us on those same sidewalks, but only traces of those winter evenings remained in my memory now— a sense of dark and cold in the street, and glittering fantasy inside.

I walked along block after block, remembering the throngs with their shopping bags and umbrellas. The show windows and big clock in front of Holmes. Morrison's Cafeteria, the one that looked like a Spanish patio, and the restaurant mezzanine in the big Walgreens store. Farther down Canal, a Woolworth's that smelled like floor-cleaning compound, Evening in Paris, and popcorn. A streetcar passed, and I remembered how they jerked and bucked, their clanging bell, and the electric smell of them in the rain.

I glanced up narrow streets into the Quarter, but I wasn't ready to go back there yet. Suddenly exhausted, I took a taxi home.

All was quiet indoors. Late afternoon November dusk darkened the room. Instead of turning on a lamp, I dropped my shopping bags and lay down on the couch for a few minutes before making dinner.

A twelve-year-old girl stands in the hallway a foot or two from the open door of her parents' room. She hears her mother's voice: "Manda, maybe you'll make a quiet marriage when you're older and looks don't matter as much. But you're not pretty like Nita. She'll probably marry young. I'm sure you'll do well in college and have a wonderful career."

The girl backs quietly away from the door. She knows her mother is trying to drive a wedge between her and her sister. Her only chance of preventing it is to never admit she heard.

I woke, confused. Were the voices ghosts or a dream? It hardly mattered. It wasn't the first time I'd heard those words, or variations on the same theme.

The sister who could hope for nothing but a career, the one who could only marry. Mine wasn't the only family I knew of that typecast its kids. "The pretty one," "the smart one," "the athletic one," and "the talented one" were tiresomely commonplace descriptions.

Parents who pigeonholed their children this way were blind to their real gifts. I'd made as good grades as Manda, but she was "the smart one," so mine hadn't counted. And what right did Mom have to say I was prettier? We were ourselves. A perfect Manda and a perfect Nita, the only ones who'd ever exist. Why couldn't our parents recognize a miracle when they saw one?

Anger brought me fully awake. I blundered to my feet in the dark and switched on a lamp.

I turned and gasped. Dietrich.

I'd become blasé about ghosts, but this one looked real. He couldn't be, of course, because he'd be almost seventy if he was alive. I hung on to that thought and waited to see what he'd do.

He stood in the doorway to the foyer as he had the last time I'd seen him, cradling his injured right hand in his left. Twenty-five years old, he'd been, and God, he looked like a kid.

Within seconds, he began to disappear. Not like the others, though—he faded in layers. First his clothes so he stood naked, then his flesh, and finally, a skeleton that slowly dissolved to nothing.

17

I backed down the hallway in horror. Goosebumps chased over my whole body in waves. Fleeing into my bedroom, I slammed and locked the door. Totally illogical, since it would do nothing to stop the ghosts, but it felt comforting just the same.

I slept with my plush kangaroo that night, for the first time since I was about eight years old. Not that I slept much. But sometime in the night, I made a decision: I wasn't a child anymore. This time, I had a say in what happened.

In the morning, fortified with a couple of cups of strong coffee, I called a meeting of the ghosts. Didn't matter whether they existed only in my mind or not. It was time to talk to them. And I'd had most of the night to think about what to say.

Taking a seat on the couch, I dinged a knife on the side of a glass of water, the way my boss had done in the lunchroom at work before she made an announcement.

"Okay, guys," I said. "Last night was over the top. No need for the amateur theatrics—you already have my attention. Dial it down. Next time any of you pull something like that, I'll have a big yellow bulldozer in the yard the very next day. Roar, crash, rip, splinter. Backup beeper, and on she comes again. It'll take about an hour. No more house. *I'll* have someplace else to go. You won't.

"And Dietrich, if that was a none-too-subtle way of letting me know you're dead, it was unnecessary. The way you lived, you had a one-way ticket to the paupers' cemetery, and a short ride at that. You probably never reached thirty. And if you think I care, you're even crazier dead than you were when you were alive.

"Lay low for a while, all of you. Don't push your luck—I mean it."

I dressed, put on my new coat, and walked out.

A storm had come through in the night, and the world was cold and soggy. A mean wind tested my new warm clothes, but I was mostly pleased with the way they kept it out. I shoved my hands deep in my pockets—I'd forgotten to buy gloves. A soft, warm scarf would be an improvement, too. Luckily, they'd be easy to find now—Christmas shopping season was getting into full swing. I could probably find something in the neighborhood.

On an impulse, I knocked at Mary's door. She opened it, dressed in a fluffy pink robe.

"Oh, I'm sorry," I said. "I thought you'd be up and about."

"Come on in," she said, stepping back. "It's not early for me—I was just too lazy to dress yet this morning. Come in and have some hot coffee. Lord, it's cold."

She took my coat and I sat in her kitchen while she fussed with the coffeepot.

"I'm so glad you dropped by," she said. "I never did remember to ask for your phone number, and I wanted to invite you for Thanksgiving. We won't have a lot of people—only Al and me and our daughter. She's younger than you, so you probably wouldn't have known her when you were growing up."

"Oh, thanks . . . but I was going to ask a friend of mine to come to my place. I think she's alone, and maybe she doesn't have other plans."

"Well, invite her here. You girls will have a good time. Who is she?"

"Her name's Enid Stone. She's the librarian at the branch at the shopping center. Maybe you've seen her—tall, light brown hair, around forty years old?"

"Haven't been to the library since my daughter was little, and I'm not much of a reader," Mary said. "but I'm sure your friend is nice. You ask her, and we'll have a good dinner together. I know my daughter would like to meet both of you."

"Thanks, then," I said. "I'll ask her and let you know. Can I bring something?"

"You just bring yourselves," she said.

She poured our coffee into her thick cups. I sipped, letting the warmth and caffeine feel like steam clearing my head.

"How've you been?" she asked.

A truthful answer wouldn't do, so I said, "I'm doing fine. Bought some new winter clothes yesterday. Canal Street sure has changed a lot."

"Oh, you don't want to go to Canal Street to shop anymore," she said. "We always go to Lakeside Mall. Was that here when you left?"

"Yes," I said. "It's probably much bigger now. But I don't drive."

"Why, of all things! Your dad didn't teach you when you were a teenager?"

"No," I said. "He was old-fashioned. He thought women shouldn't drive. I'm planning to take driving lessons in the spring."

She laughed. "Even Al's not *that* old-fashioned," she said.

"Is he home?" I asked. "I didn't mean to interrupt if you're busy."

"Oh, he's out in his shop. He has a heater out there and everything. Tries to make it as comfortable as the house. He always has a project. Cleaning the place up when he's finished with one job gives him ideas about what he wants to do next. He even has a sign out there: 'NOTHING HAS A SHORTER LIFE THAN A CLEAN SHOP.' Makes me laugh."

She looked around her immaculate kitchen. "I used to be that way with cooking. Nothing inspired me more than to have everything clean and ready to use. But now, well, I've been the chief cook for so many years—I like to take a break for a while."

We chatted a while longer, then I thanked her for the coffee and got up to leave.

"Wait," she said. "Let me get a pencil and paper for your phone number. I'll call and give you the time and so on for Thanksgiving. I'll give you mine, too."

She tore a strip of paper off the bottom of her grocery list, wrote her phone number on it, and handed it to me. When I'd stuffed it in my pocket and dictated mine to her, I put on my coat and continued my walk.

It had gotten warmer. The temperature was about the same—it was still gusty and damp, the sky was still gray. All the same, it had gotten warmer.

18

The ghosts did take a short break, but my drawing went on. One picture showed me—probably about age nine—playing with my paper dolls. I'd decided I liked the face of one doll better, but preferred another's posture and clothes. So I carefully cut their heads off and swapped them. Looking at the picture, I felt an odd rush of affection, thinking what a funny kid I'd been. Dr. Frankenstein meets Betsy McCall.

Another, from about the same time—Bob, my pet mouse. I had loved that tiny creature, and insisted I was a mouse, too. Again, a moment of tenderness for my child self.

Another showed Manda and me making pizza. It must have been the last year before she left for college. I'd only seen her a few times since then—she lived a thousand miles from anyone in the family. We'd written and phoned only occasionally—but that was a lot more contact than I'd had with Lou.

Then I started drawing pictures of things I hadn't seen—Manda's college graduation, her wedding, her children. Lou as a grown man. All the things I'd walked away from.

What if I hadn't?

What if I'd worked my way through college or gotten scholarships? Gotten a job I enjoyed? One that came with vacation days, so I could have visited relatives once in a while? Stayed in touch, taken the bad with the good? Wasn't that what people normally did?

Frustrated with my drawings and the way they made me feel, I put down my pencil and spoke to the air.

"I don't want to do this anymore," I said. "Take your damned drawings and shove them."

I turned on my computer and checked my email.

———

Date: November 15, 2003 9:18 AM
To: Juanita Jenkins
From: Louis J. Jenkins
Subject: Re: Pax

Fair enough. Let's start over. I'm not happy about the way things turned out. So I'd like to ask you—and I sincerely mean this in a non-nasty way: Why did you inherit almost everything Dad had, while Manda and I were left out in the cold? No accusations, but I'd like to know.

Lou

———

Date: November 15, 2003 11:28 AM
To: Louis J. Jenkins
From: Juanita Jenkins
Subject: Re: Pax

Dear Lou,

You were eleven years old when I left home.
Over the years, I think I sent you a couple
of birthday cards, maybe even a Christmas
present once or twice. I never heard jack from

(Delete.)

Did it occur to you that I might have needed
help with Dad sometime in the past few

(Delete.)

How did *you* make *your* break? After Dad put
you through college, did you sort of drift away,
or what? Was it gradual, or did something

(Delete.)

Did you hurt as much as I did? What made you change from the golden child to someone who didn't bother

(Delete.)

I'm sorry you see it as being left out in the cold. I think it had nothing to do with Dad's feelings about any of us. I think he was being practical. You and Manda both have houses and also jobs that have brought you a good income. I don't have either. That's mostly my own fault, but maybe in the end, he was just trying to make sure we all did okay, regardless of the past.

Mom's will was the same as his, by the way. I didn't even know their wishes. I hadn't seen either Dad or Mom for decades before they made their wills.

I wish they'd written letters to all of us to explain, and maybe they would have eventually. Mom died unexpectedly, and Dad was much further into dementia by that time than she'd let anyone know.

So "practicality" is a guess. We can all
speculate forever, but I doubt if we'd come
up with anything better. If you'd like to have any
possessions of Dad's or Mom's, or any family
memorabilia like photos that are still
in the house, I'd be happy to send them to
you.

Why don't we plan to get together and get
reacquainted? Maybe Manda will come, too—
would that work? Maybe sometime during the
holidays, if you don't have other plans? Or
afterward, if you do.

Love,
Nita

————

Date: November 15, 2003 12:01 PM
To: Amanda Lowe
From: Juanita Jenkins
Subject: Holidays?

Dear Manda,

I know this sounds off-the-wall, but the
house seems to be haunted. I'm sure I'm not
imagining it and reasonably sure I'm not losing

(Delete.)

I'm wondering if you'd like to come and visit
sometime during the holidays, or afterward if
that would work better for you. Miss you.

Love,
Nita

———————

Maybe they'd come. Probably, they wouldn't see
the ghosts, but at least they'd see me, meet my friends,
and judge for themselves whether I looked or acted
like a nutcase.

Now that I'd invited them to visit, I realized I needed
furniture for their rooms, maybe rugs. I needed to paint
the bedrooms and living room, too. I had to get rid
of Dad's sickroom equipment and boxes and boxes of
old papers. I had a long to-do list, and I was going to
have to do it all myself. Ghosts and workmen weren't
a combination I'd be eager to see.

First of all, I'd have to get rid of the stupid drawings. I didn't want Lou and Manda to see them, and I didn't want to see them myself. Deciding to throw them away, I grabbed the wastebasket and went looking for them. But I didn't find a single one. They were gone.

———

Date: November 18, 2003 4:07 PM
To: Juanita Jenkins
From: Louis J. Jenkins
Subject: Re: Pax

Dear Nita,

I see what you mean. And I don't need anything, so it was wrong of me to make a big deal out of the will. I felt slighted—dumb. Sorry.

It's been decades since I saw you. Can we make this a special occasion? Do you have plans for Christmas Eve and/or Christmas Day? It would be great to spend them with you.

Love,
Lou

———————

Date: November 19, 2003 8:16 AM
To: Juanita Jenkins
From: Amanda Lowe
Subject: Re: Holidays?

Hi Nita,

I talked to Lou—Is Christmas Eve or Christmas
Day really okay with you? I'd love to do it. The
kids are so grown up now. They have their own
plans, and Ben doesn't care one way or the
other. He says he'll wait and celebrate a fancy
New Year's Eve with me! Looking forward to
both events.

Love,
Manda

19

Dad had kept his records in order until about five years before he died, and everything after that was chaos. I divided them between two boxes, one for financial records, one for everything else. When I finished, I closed the box of financial papers and set it aside. I'd put it in chronological order later and take it to the accountant. I couldn't tell what to save and what I could throw away.

Next were photos and negatives. For a while, Dad had a good camera, and he developed black-and-white negatives and prints at night in the bathroom. The camera was gone—probably he'd sold it at some point, when he needed money to pay creditors who couldn't be stiffed.

The pictures were beautiful. He'd been talented, and had tried to go professional. But his photography business had failed just like every other one before it. Now, I looked with bewilderment at portraits of us as children. Somehow, he'd lost the love that shone from them, packed it away in a cardboard box, forgotten as old bank statements and unpaid bills.

I kept coming back to one set of photos of Manda, Lou, and me on Christmas morning. Sitting near the tree, opening our presents. Our smiles and shining eyes were captured forever. But Dad was gone, and the love that inspired those photos had died long before he did. How had he turned into a man who threw Christmas in the dump, every last elf and star, every last shred of tinsel?

I pushed the box of photos aside.

With two more empty boxes, I sorted for any records that had to do with Dad's last business venture, the successful one. After I'd left home, he'd invented several toys that caught on and made enormous amounts of money. Manda had told me about it at the time, but I'd dismissed it as ironic: How could a man who disliked children have invented amazing toys?

Now I remembered he had made that rocking horse. And bunny shadows on the wall, and a herd of charming animals he sculpted for us out of multicolored telephone wire. I remembered more and more. He hadn't *started* as a man who disliked children.

And Mom. When had she changed from the cake baker, the most beautiful woman in the world, to the one who screamed that she wished we didn't exist?

I remembered what the ghosts had shown me, and more. The miscarriage. The finally fulfilled longing for a son, followed by gut-level battles about what a son should be. Years of failure and scarcity, dinners of scraps, our filthy house, neighbors who shunned us. Anger feeding accusation in a vicious circle.

Beyond that, the truth was as tantalizing as a mirage. Why did their marriage go bad? Which of them had started it? Trying to figure that one out was like watching a tennis match. She did this because he said that, because she said that, because he did this . . . back and forth, back and forth . . .

I grinned suddenly, remembering Lou's description of tennis—"the kind of thing a cat would watch."

It was unsolvable. Whatever had gone wrong between Mom and Dad had gone *disastrously* wrong. War had been declared, and as in all wars, there was "collateral damage." Which was military-speak for what happens to innocent bystanders. Like kids.

Maybe a psychologist could have unwound the tangle, but Mom and Dad were too proud and too poor to see one. It was far beyond me—and anyway, who was I to analyze any relationship? I'd chosen to be alone. Had lived without roommates, friends, lovers, children. Had walked by myself like a solitary bear. I knew nothing about being close to other people.

Except at work, where I spent my days talking to the people I took care of—old people with regrets and family quarrels, lovers and enemies. I'd handed them tissues when they wept, and tried to console them for their failures. For the sons and daughters who didn't visit, for their own physical weaknesses and incontinence. Their losses and humiliations. For fear of death, sometimes—less often than I would have thought, though. I'd heard it all. I knew how life looks at the end of people's stories, just before they close the back cover of the book. But as far as having a life of my own was concerned, I'd done nothing.

Mulling it over wasn't getting me anywhere. I turned back to my home-remodeling projects, hoping to avoid the past by concentrating on ordinary tasks.

My flurry of shopping had furnished all the things I needed to spruce up Lou's and Manda's rooms, but actually doing it was like stepping into the lives they'd lived there. I didn't *see* their ghosts—I *felt* them. In a sense, I became my brother and sister. As empty as their rooms were of possessions, they were filled with old thoughts and feelings. Manda, the valedictorian, who was led to believe she was ugly. Sadly looking in her mirror to see if Mom was right, if she should forget about dating, marriage, children—anything except a career. Lou, losing himself in the strange worlds of *National Geographic* to get away from the stranger one outside his bedroom door. Sadly looking in his mirror to see if Dad was right, if he was a baby, a mama's boy, a wimp.

Both of them doing without the sister who blew up like a bomb. Manda had been away at college by then, but maybe Lou had needed a friend—and I'd walked out on him as well as everyone else. True, he'd been a nasty little boy—but maybe I could have tipped the balance another way? I didn't know—I hadn't tried.

Had Mom and Dad reached a truce after the last business succeeded? But, except for ending the money troubles, how could that have mattered to a kid at the eye of their personal hurricane? Success had surely come too late. If you make it clear when you're poor that you can't stand your family, how do you take it back when you're rich? No wonder Lou seemed hung up on money now.

And Manda—she'd escaped in an approved way, but she'd had to hide who she was and where she came from—among people who couldn't have imagined a home where the floors were carpeted with cat shit. She'd started off as a scholarship and loan student, working in the school cafeteria to pay for books. Then Dad struck it rich, and her way had been paid; she could afford to buy clothes and shoes like the other girls, could fit in, at least superficially. But behind the façade, she was different, and she had to have known it.

Despite Mom's prediction, Manda had married. In fact, she'd gotten engaged to the son of a man Dad had known in the army. When she'd told him that, with a kind of "small world" delight, he insisted it couldn't be so.

"Can't be the same guy," he said. "The guy I knew was Jewish."

He stared blankly at her when she told him her fiancé was, indeed, Jewish. He and Mom didn't go to the wedding—said it was too far away. When Manda and Ben had kids, a reconciliation had been reached, but on her side, it was a brittle and bitter one.

When the painting was done, I washed the windows, hung new curtains, and put down rugs. After that, they were nothing but empty rooms, waiting for furniture.

Then I took a break. The hallways, kitchen, dining room, and living room could wait till after Thanksgiving.

I could hardly believe Lou and Manda had chosen me to spend the holiday with—I hadn't really hoped they could rearrange their lives that much. But they were coming. That meant I had a month to get the place in shape.

If there were any way to put ghosts to work, I could have assembled a whole construction crew. But as it was, all I had was me.

20

I looked through my closet for something to wear to Mary's dinner, and wished I'd been more extravagant the day I'd gone downtown. Unless I could find something presentable in the local shops, I'd have to go again.

Still, why not? With Lou and Manda coming for Christmas, I wanted to buy a few gifts anyway. I chewed my lower lip, thinking about the sort of gifts I'd like to get them—Saks Fifth Avenue at Canal Place wouldn't do. I'd have to visit the specialty boutiques of the French Quarter. Remembering the cool little fool I'd been, bopping around the Quarter like jailbait on steroids, I wasn't sure I could face it.

At fifteen, I'd explored the narrow streets and thought of them as "my place." I spent every afternoon there—homework at public school wasn't enough of a challenge, after my years in the segregation academy, for me to give a second thought to wasting most of my time. And Mom and Dad couldn't have cared less where I went or how late I stayed out—might not have minded if I'd quit coming home altogether.

And as Mom had mentioned in her scornful monologues to Manda, I was pretty. The artists were soon using me as a shill to attract portrait customers, then as a clothed model for drawing classes. But, though they might flirt mildly with an attractive girl, they were too smart to cross the legal line with a minor.

All except Dietrich.

An epileptic who rarely bothered to take medicine, Dietrich embraced his disability as an excuse to do whatever he wanted—he genuinely believed the world owed him endless compensation. Whether he was legally insane was impossible for me, as a layperson, to say. But regardless, he was serious bad news.

At the time I met him, so was I. Desperate for love from anyone, loyal far beyond a fault, clueless about dealing with surges of adult hormones, I was out of control.

My memories made me hot with humiliation. And then with accusation, as I sorted through my feelings. For the first time, I asked: What parent of a troubled teenager just turns her loose and shrugs? Dietrich and my parents were adults. I was a kid, and I was the one who paid most.

I went out to the kitchen to console myself with a cup of coffee. The house was still and warm. Almost stuffy. On impulse, I decided to go to town right then and get it over with. Shopping for Lou and Manda would be fun, even if I did have to go to the Quarter. I headed back to my room to get ready.

Coming out of the bathroom into the hall, a fifteen-year-old girl pauses. The sound of the toilet flushing has brought her father and mother to their bedroom door.

"It's over?" her mother says.

She nods. She feels a drench of blood on her sanitary napkin. She starts to go back in the bathroom, but her mother lays a hand on her arm.

"It wasn't really a baby," her mother says. "Just a kind of organized blood clot."

"I'll have you know, that woman charged five hundred dollars," her father says.

They vanished as quickly as the snap of a camera shutter.

I stood shakily in the hallway. Ghosts or no ghosts, I didn't think I could live in this house much longer. But if I sold it to strangers, would they get a replay of this whole sordid story? Sarah had suggested that no one else could see the ghosts, but how would she know?

I'd threatened the ghosts that I'd have the house torn down, but I wasn't sure that would work. If I built another one on the lot, would they come to the housewarming? Or—why would they even stay in one place? Would I see Dietrich everywhere I went for the rest of my life? Was I in fact losing my mind?

I pushed the feelings away. If Sarah and Enid were right, this personal movie had a point. Once that point was made, the show would be over. In the meantime, I intended to reclaim the French Quarter. I refused to cower in my house because of what I'd been or done more than forty years ago.

Downtown, I started with the mall. This time, less cautious than before, I bought several nice outfits. Loaded with shopping bags, I strolled into the Quarter like a wealthy tourist who'd never been there before.

On a cold, damp day in November, few street artists were working. No paintings on black velvet hung from the wrought-iron fences of the St. Louis Cathedral or Jackson Square. The portrait sketchers and cartoonists had stayed home. With long-forgotten skill, I evaded panhandlers, looking for shops. Almost all the ones I remembered were gone.

There was barely a vestige of the streets I'd known. The buildings were still standing, of course—this was a historic district, jealously preserved. But the familiar shops had been replaced by new merchants, new fashions, new people. A fancy patisserie had become a health-food store. A former gumbo restaurant now featured tapas. In this old place, everything was new.

I remembered something I'd read a long time before—that within a few years, every cell in the body changes. If that was true, not only were these not the same scenes, but I wasn't the same person—not physically, anyway.

Not mentally or emotionally, either, I knew. So my memories of those other streetscapes, that other Nita, had no more substance than my ghosts at home.

At random, I picked an antique shop. Inside, it was dim, with a familiar smell of furniture polish. Typical Royal Street inventory. China, silver, jewelry—none of that would work for Manda and Lou. Furniture, silk fans, mirrors, celluloid dresser sets, silver picture frames.

Picture frames?

I selected three, paid, and waited while the clerk wrapped them neatly in tissue paper. Thanking her, I left, hailed the first cruising cab, and went home to Metairie.

That night, I dreamed I was in a cage, like one of the big cages at the Audubon Park Zoo. Everyone I'd ever been angry with was packed in there with me, standing room only, and all of them between me and the door. Family, schoolmates, Dietrich, a few people in Los Angeles—no one was missing. I could make the door open whenever I wanted, but if I did, they'd all escape before I could get out. And they deserved to be in a cage—I didn't.

21

When I tried on my new outfits back in my bedroom at home, the "prettiness" Mom had been so scathing about to Manda flashed back at me from the mirror. Good God, I was nearly old enough to draw Social Security, and *that* was still there?

For most of my life, I'd kept a lid on it. Dressed more than modestly—frumpishly, in fact. I hadn't used makeup. I'd worn my hair in a ponytail and kept it natural when it started to go silver. As far as I was concerned, beauty was for people who wanted to attract other people. I didn't.

I'd been astonished when someone I knew told me I must have had an easy life because I was so good-looking. What easy life? I'd worked at a hard job, pouring out love to sad, helpless people. It had made me happy to be able to do it, but I'd never thought I'd been favored because I looked the way women were supposed to look. She offended me when she said that—it felt like theft of something I'd earned.

I'd bought the new clothes as a gesture of respect for Mary's celebration. But they made me into a model in an ad directed at aging, upper-class women—estate planning, maybe, or wrinkle cream. I hoped my friends wouldn't admire the getup too much or take it as a sign that I'd changed.

I stuck out my tongue at the lovely lady in the mirror, changed back to jeans and sweatshirt, and went back to sorting Dad's papers.

Among his early files, I found manila envelopes labeled with Manda's, Lou's, and my names. Birth certificates, school records and photos, some medical records. I set my brother's and sister's envelopes aside to give them when they visited. Probably they already had copies of all the important records, but whether they wanted any of this was up to them.

My own envelope contained the same kind of thing. But also, among the dull, miscellaneous papers was the money order I'd sent Dad without explanation a year or so after I left home, as soon as I could scrape the five hundred dollars together. He had never cashed it.

A cold, desolate feeling filled me. I turned and left the room, still holding the little piece of paper that had once been my justification, my revenge.

A man struggles in the hallway outside his girlfriend's room, his hand pinned in a slammed door. He'd tried to force his way in, but now all he wants is to leave. She won't release him. She leans her whole body weight against the door. With her fist, she pounds the fingers that project through the crack, trying to do as much damage to his hand as possible. He yells, she pounds, he struggles. The noise brings her father into the hallway.

"Stop, Nita," her father says. "Let go."

She does. Her father stands back as she opens the door. As her boyfriend retreats to the living room, she follows a few steps behind. He stops at the foyer and turns toward her, cradling his injured right hand in his left. His expression is accusing.

Before he can say a word, she flings a gold ring set with a tiny diamond directly at his face and runs back to her room, slamming the door behind her. He turns toward the foyer again, beginning to fade.

"Wait," I said to the ghost. Becoming more solid, he faced me.

"Dietrich," I said, "I was fifteen years old; you were twenty-five. Legally, you were a rapist."

He stood expressionless, listening.

I went on. "I know you were sick. I'm not sure even the law would have held you accountable. But did it occur to you that what you did was wrong?"

He stood quietly, not saying yes or no.

"Even if you meant well, you did something inexcusable. You took advantage of a reckless, desperate teenager. I was sick, too."

Again, no movement, nothing. I took a deep breath and went on.

"There was no way you could have been anything but a disaster for me. My parents should have stopped it. But they were no saner than we were. *All* of us were wrong. Wherever you are, whatever you are, can we let the past bury itself?"

He seemed to consider for a moment. Then he nodded once, turned, and left, closing the front door gently behind him.

I didn't look to see whether he disappeared right away. I hoped he didn't. I imagined him walking up the street toward the bus stop, going home.

I sat on the couch for a long time. I got up only when something on the floor drew my attention—the gleam of the gold ring.

22

I spent the days before Thanksgiving in a flurry of cleaning, painting, sorting, and dragging discards out to the porch for the thrift store. I called them so often, I wondered if they were beginning to recognize my voice.

I bought everything I still needed for Lou's and Manda's rooms, and replacements for worn pieces elsewhere that I'd given away. I let the stores deliver it and set it up, mentally daring the ghosts to show their faces. They didn't.

I finished sorting Dad's papers and junk. Finally, I had nothing left to clean but my own room.

I'd been living in there for years now, mostly using it only for sleeping. The box with the books was the only one I'd opened.

Reluctantly, I started on the mess in the closet. Most of the boxes held nothing but workbooks, papers, and school supplies. One had a pair of dry, cracked shoes, a moldy purse, and a few plastic horses. Some had old clothes, hair rollers, or unmatched socks. Mom must have packed the boxes, because I certainly wouldn't have saved most of this clutter. Even the thrift store wouldn't want junk like this. The only treasures were the ones I'd unpacked earlier—the plush kangaroo and the chambered nautilus.

I gazed at my shell in its newly repaired stand on the dresser, admiring it as I so often had as a teenager. The shell was halved to show its inner compartments, and polished like mother-of-pearl. I'd hated to leave it behind when I left home, but there was no way to take such a fragile thing with me.

I had often reached a peaceful, almost meditative state just looking at it, thinking of it in its home somewhere deep in the sea, floating in blue-green infinity. Sometimes I'd run my finger over edges of compartments the nautilus had created and abandoned as it grew. I pictured it as a house with deserted rooms, a sealed-over past.

By the day before Thanksgiving, the house was looking good. I spent much of that day making a loaf of French bread for Mary's dinner. Enid phoned once to ask what I was wearing, and I told her about my new clothes.

The next afternoon, I dressed for Mary's party, hoping I didn't look too fancy. I wore the ring—it was a lovely one, a beautifully sculpted gold rose with a diamond dewdrop at its center. Once, it would have felt unbearably creepy to even touch it. Now I regarded it as another gift from time.

I wrapped my loaf of bread and left the house. It was a chilly day, but not too cold for a short walk. All the trees were bare except the live oaks, and most of the gardens were stark and dull. The streets and sidewalks were all but empty—everyone else had reached their destinations, everyone else had begun their holiday. And in a few minutes, so did I.

I was the last to arrive. Al took my coat, and apart from a few comments on the order of "You look great," no one seemed concerned about my transformation.

I met Mary's daughter, Melissa. Enid had already introduced herself to the others.

It was a wonderful, traditional Thanksgiving dinner. Afterward, Enid, Melissa, and I cleaned up, insisting that Mary relax in the living room. I wasn't sure how relaxing it was for her to watch football with Al, but it was the best we could do.

It was dark when I left with a tote bag of leftovers. I walked home, feeling wonderful about my new friends. It was very cold, and I huddled inside my pretty coat, planning to go back to town and buy a down jacket in the Christmas sales, if any stores in New Orleans had them. Otherwise, I'd find one online. Warmth trumped beauty, as far as I was concerned.

As I approached my house, I was humming "We Gather Together," an old memory from my church school days.

A young woman walks stealthily down the front path of her house. As she reaches the sidewalk, she pauses to look back just once. Adjusting her rucksack, she heads toward the highway, where she'll thumb a ride. First to Baton Rouge, then across the country, step by step, to California. Soon she'll have the only job she can find, working as an assistant in a Los Angeles rest home. She'll stay there for the next forty years.

She crosses the street and either vanishes or is lost in the darkness beneath the Miss America Block's tunnel of trees.

"Au revoir," I said softly.

23

The Christmas tree stood in the corner where we'd always put them. I hadn't been able to match the old fluorescent ball lights we'd had, but I'd come as close as I could. Shopping on auction sites on the Internet, I'd found duplicates of most of the glass ornaments that Manda had mourned. I'd saved the boxes to pack them in so she could take them home with her.

It was fun.

Under the tree were three packages "from Santa Claus." Of course, I knew what was in them, since I was Santa. I was hoping Manda and Lou wouldn't be able to guess what was inside the shiny gold paper.

And I hoped they'd be the only gifts. I'd told my brother and sister I didn't want anything, that having them come see me was the most wonderful gift I could imagine. I'd insisted, and they'd agreed, if only reluctantly.

Since I wasn't expecting packages, I was surprised when the mail carrier rang the bell on December 23. But it wasn't a package. I signed for the registered letter he'd handed me, and he wished me a happy holiday before going on his way.

Opening it, I found a legal document from the city. It said that the dead-end street that stopped at my back fence would be extended to intersect with the street my house faced on. My property was to be expropriated for public use, and further details about the process would be forthcoming. I would be paid fair market value. An attached document contained instructions in case I wanted to appeal.

I stood in shock for a moment. And then I thought, how apt. The house's story was finished, and now, like one of its ghosts, it would disappear.

But I wouldn't disappear—not again. I decided to buy another home in the neighborhood, to not lose the friends I'd made here. I'd live in a place with no clinging memories, and I'd plant Mary's roses in the yard.

When Lou and Manda came on Christmas Eve, after the hugs and the exclamations over the Christmas tree, I told them.

"But you've worked so hard!" Manda said. "The place looks wonderful. They can't just tear it down!"

"Can you fight it?" Lou asked.

I shook my head. "It's fine," I said. "I plan to stay in the neighborhood, but this house isn't important to me. In fact, it might be better to start new."

They nodded. I wasn't sure they understood at all— possibly they didn't care one way or the other. I'd told them nothing about the ghosts, so I could hardly have expected them to accept what a relief it was that the house was being demolished. But their memories of the place were probably as confused and painful as mine, ghosts or no ghosts.

"It's fine," I said again.

After dinner, we gathered around the tree and listened to Christmas carols on the radio. Then I gave them their gifts and opened my own. Three copies of Dad's best Christmas photo in the silver frames I'd bought for them.

As we laughed and reminisced, I suddenly noticed a movement between us and the tree—and so did they.

A father focuses his camera on his children as they open presents beside the Christmas tree. The children smile without being prompted, happy and excited by their gifts from Santa. Behind his camera, the photographer is tender and loving, enchanted by his own miraculous gift— the gift of being these children's father. His wife stands near him, smiling at their smiles.

Slowly, all five of them disappeared, and the lights of the tree shone again on an empty space.

"My God," Lou said. "What was that?"

Manda looked stunned, almost beyond speech. Then, glancing at her gift, she cried, "It's the photo! How did you do that, Nita?"

"I'm sorry." I said. "I didn't do it. I've been seeing scenes from our lives since Dad died. But I thought it was over."

"Why didn't you tell us?" Manda said.

"How could you have believed it? If someone else had told me a story like that, I'd have thought they were hallucinating. But I'm glad I saw them. I learned a lot. I'm glad you saw them, too."

After more talk, more explanations—and a couple of rounds of cognac—they turned in. I wished them good night, and returned to the living room to tidy a bit and unplug the strings of lights.

The parents stand together beside the Christmas tree after all the presents have been opened. They stare silently, almost pleadingly, at their middle-aged daughter, and she remembers how her father sometimes seemed to want to tell her something after he'd lost all his words. And how he would turn away in frustration, sometimes in tears. Too much to say, too late to say anything.

Without knowing why, I was sure this was the last time I'd ever see them. "Don't worry," I told them. "I know. It's okay now. I'm okay. And I'm sorry, too."

And then I let them go.

ANNE L. WATSON, a retired historic preservation architecture consultant, is the author of several novels, plus books on such diverse subjects as soapmaking and baking with cookie molds. A former resident of New Orleans—the setting of *A Chambered Nautilus*—she currently lives in Bellingham, Washington, with her husband and fellow author, Aaron Shepard. You can find her online at **www.annelwatson.com**.

www.ingramcontent.com/pod-product-compliance
Lightning Source LLC
Chambersburg PA
CBHW052207170626
46812CB00004B/1686